WILLOW VALLEY

Birthday Fun

Tracey Corderoy

Illustrated by Hannah Whitty

First published in the UK in 2012 by Scholastic Children's Books
An imprint of Scholastic Ltd
Euston House, 24 Eversholt Street
London, NW1 1DB, UK
Registered office: Westfield Road, Southam, Warwickshire, CV47 0RA
SCHOLASTIC and associated logos are trademarks and/
or registered trademarks of Scholastic Inc.

Text copyright © Tracey Corderoy, 2012
Illustration copyright © Hannah Whitty, 2012

The rights of Tracey Corderoy and Hannah Whitty to be identified as the
author and illustrator of this work have been asserted by them.

Cover illustration © Hannah Whitty, 2012

ISBN 978 1 407 12474 2

A CIP catalogue record for this book
is available from the British Library

Printed and bound by CPI Group Ltd (UK), Croydon, CR0 4YY
Papers used by Scholastic Children's Books
are made from wood grown in sustainable forests.

1 3 5 7 9 10 8 6 4 2

This is a work of fiction. Names, characters, places, incidents
are products of the author's imagination or are used
fictitiously. Any resemblance to actual people, living or dead,
events or locales is entirely coincidental.

www.scholastic.co.uk/zone
traceycorderoy.com

For Charlotte, with my love always. . .

T.C xx

WILLOW VALLEY

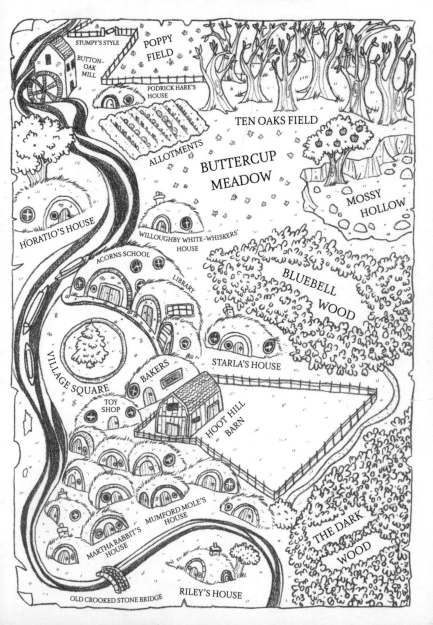

Chapter 1

Riley woke from a deep sleep with a big, fluffy wriggle. "Ahhhh. . ." yawned the scruffy little mouse, snuffling into his pillow.

He rubbed his eyes to clear the sleepy dust that had glued them shut. Then he rolled over and gazed at the ceiling.

Slowly a smile spread across Riley's face, stretching from whisker to whisker, as he suddenly remembered what day it was. Today was his *birthday*. At last!

Riley sat up and his tiny pink nose sniff, sniff, sniffed the air. All was quiet. He must be the first one awake.

Ribbons of shimmering light crept through the thick stone window, casting bright streaks on to his bedroom walls. It was going to be a clear spring day.

C-r-r-e-e-a-k. Riley's heavy bedroom door opened and a short, plump mouse carrying lots of presents shuffled in.

Riley's mum had twinkly eyes and her coat was thick and shiny. She was chocolate brown, much darker than Riley, whose fur was the colour of toffee. "Happy birthday!" she called brightly.

"Oooh!" gasped Riley. *"Presents!"*

He wriggled out of his thick wool blankets and knelt up on the bed. This was going to be the best birthday ever! Later on, he was having a party on the *Whirligig* – the biggest of the Willow Valley narrowboats.

Riley could just imagine it, all done up with rows of colourful bunting.

There would be presents and games and a birthday cake dotted with flickering candles! He and his friends were going to have so much fun.

As his mum laid Riley's presents on his bed, a tiny white mouse scampered into the room. She was wearing a sparkly tiara and clutching a small, bent wand. "*Riley, wait!*" squeaked his sister, Mimi-Rose. "*I* want to see your presents!"

She clambered up Riley's blankets and plonked herself down beside her big brother. "*Oooh!*" she cried excitedly. "I *wish* it was *my* birthday!"

Riley gazed down at his presents.

They'd been beautifully wrapped in big, shiny leaves and tied with trails of ivy. Some had bunches of fir cones sitting neatly on the top, whilst others had clusters of bright red berries.

Bursting with excitement, Riley picked one up and pulled off its ivy ribbon. The big rhubarb leaf fell open and he lifted out the present inside.

It was a long stripey scarf that his mum had made herself. They'd collected the wool off the hedgerows last summer. Then she'd spun it, and dyed it with autumn berries in shades of blues and purples. She'd knitted it on cold winter

nights when Riley and Mimi-Rose had
been tucked up in bed.

"Thanks!" said Riley, putting it on.
This scarf would come in useful. Even
though spring had just arrived, icy
winds still whipped through the valley.

"What else have you got?" squeaked Mimi-Rose.

"Let's see!" said Riley. And one by one, he opened his other presents. . .

His sister had painted him a picture, though he wasn't quite sure of what!

"*You!*" she cried, prodding a splodge that looked like a hairy raindrop. "And that's me in my tiara!"

"Of course," grinned Riley. "Err, *thanks!*"

Grandpa's gift was a wooden train set with signals, flags and a driver.

"He spent hours making it!" Riley's mum smiled.

Riley also got a spinning top, a shiny bell for his bike and a jam jar filled with berries, seeds and rings of sweet, dried apple.

Now there was only one present left to open. Riley felt along the leafy wrapping. Whatever was in there was long and thin. *"Long and thin!"* he murmured. Maybe – no – it couldn't be! But it *did* feel just the right shape. . .

Riley tore off the leaves. *"It is!"* he cried, and his eyes widened to take in a metal detector! He picked it up. "And look!" he gasped, spotting even more goodies.

There was a pair of binoculars, a little
ball of string, a compass, a hat, a small
silver spade, a flask, and a notebook and
pencil.

"*Wow!*" cried Riley, leaping off the
bed. "A real explorer's kit! Can I go out
in the fields and try it? *Please?*"

Riley had wanted to be an explorer for
as long as he could remember, just like

his dad, Barty Black-Paw, had once been.

"Not so fast!" chuckled his mum.
"You haven't had breakfast yet!
And remember, Riley, when you go
exploring—"

"I know!" Riley replied. "I won't go
into The Dark Wood, I promise!"

His mother nodded and the little
mouse suddenly fell silent. He knew
how dangerous The Dark Wood was.
There had been stories of trees so thick
that they blocked out the sun and no
flowers could grow. So that daytime
looked as gloomy as night. So that
anyone – even the *best* explorers – could

get lost . . . for ever.

Riley had often asked about the night his dad had gone exploring in The Dark Wood. The fog had been thick. The moon milky white. And Barty Black-Paw had never returned. . .

A tiny prod from Mimi-Rose brought Riley back out of his daydream, and sent them both racing downstairs. They huddled around the kitchen table as their mum cooked a big pot of porridge.

When it was steaming hot, she ladled the porridge into bowls. Then Riley and his sister added berries and nuts and a spoonful of thick, golden honey.

"Don't forget to blow," Riley told Mimi-Rose.

"And you!" giggled his sister.

They each gave their porridge a quick blow and watched as the golden ribbons of honey swirled into little pictures. "Mine's made a moustache!" cried Riley.

"Mine looks like a worm!" squealed Mimi-Rose. Then, spoons at the ready, they both tucked in. It was so delicious!

As soon as he'd finished, Riley packed an old rucksack with his new explorer's kit. Everything except his explorer's hat, which he popped on his head. Now he was ready to go!

"Here," smiled Riley's mum, handing him a flask filled with elderflower cordial. "Oh, and don't forget this!" she said, wrapping his new scarf around him.

"Can I go too?" begged Mimi-Rose, but their mother shook her head.

"You're too little, I'm afraid," she said.

"I'll be back in time for my party!" called Riley, picking up his metal detector. He opened the door and hurried out. "See you later!"

Outside in the garden a dusting of frost twinkled on the grass like glitter. Riley took out his binoculars and peered through them.

Soon he found an odd-looking stone, which he thought looked a *bit* like a jewel. He wiped off the dirt on his toffee-coloured tummy before popping it into his rucksack.

Next he examined a set of footprints trailing through the mud. Riley wondered what animal they might belong to.

Then Riley dug a little hole and unearthed a cross-looking spider. "A new species!" he cried, whipping out his notebook to draw it.

Riley had barely sketched three legs before it scuttled off under the shed. "Hey!" he giggled. "Come back here! I haven't done your body yet."

Instead, he took out his compass and watched its little arrow spin. "Time to discover a new land, I think!"

Riley repacked his rucksack carefully and raced to the blackberry bush. Then, minding the thorns, he wriggled under it, into the field beyond.

Riley now found himself in tall, swishy grass. The field was at the top of a very high hill, and the whole of Willow Valley stretched out below.

With a happy shout, he raced down, his rucksack bumping against him. "Wheeee!" he cried as the breeze sent him faster and faster.

At the bottom of the hill, some willow trees dipped their branches into the river. Riley could hear faint gurgles as the water skipped along.

As he ran, Riley spied three narrowboats bobbing about on the river. These were the boats that took the animals on their market trips. Four times a year they'd leave Willow Valley and sail into the open countryside, stopping here and there to sell their home-made goods.

In the autumn and winter they'd sell scarves and pies, crumbles and warming stews. In the spring and summer they'd take elderflower cordial and bunches of sweet-smelling flowers and jars of jam in every flavour you could imagine!

Riley spotted the *Dragonfly*. This was the boat that stored all the goods when the animals went off on their trips. It was bottle green with a bright red door and was decorated with lacy-winged dragonflies.

Sitting behind it was the *Kingfisher*. This was the captain's boat, and it was the colour of a summer sky. A big, bright kingfisher was painted on its bow, holding a fish in its beak and looking proud.

Finally, the *Whirligig* was at the back.

This was the biggest boat and was dark blue in colour. It had funny-looking beetles and pale pink roses painted round its small square windows.

As Riley got closer, he could see lots of animals bustling about on the boats. Some were hammering down loose floorboards, while others were busily painting.

"Yo ho!" called Willoughby White-Whiskers from the deck of the *Whirligig*. "If it isn't the *birthday boy*! Happy birthday, Riley!"

"Thank you, Mr White-Whiskers!" Riley called back. "What are you doing to the boats?"

"Just a lick of paint here and a bit of mending there before our trips begin!"

"B-but. . ." stuttered Riley.

"Don't worry!" smiled the old badger, who was the captain of the fleet. "The paint will have dried by this afternoon and the *Whirligig* will look splendid! My Starla wants everything to be perfect."

He winked at Riley, who grinned back. He could always rely on Starla! She was Willoughby's granddaughter and one of Riley's best friends. Bright and clever, there was no one *quite* like Starla for sorting things out!

"Where is Starla, Mr White-Whiskers?" asked Riley.

"Here I am!" cried a little fluffy badger, popping her head round the *Whirligig*'s door. She climbed up on deck. "Happy birthday, Riley!"

"Do you want to come exploring?" he asked. "We could go to Ten Oaks Field. We *might* even find some buried

treasure!" Riley waved his metal
detector in the air.

"Oh yes, I'll come!" Starla smiled. She
clapped her paws and hurried down the
gangplank, ready for an adventure.

Chapter 2

Riley and Starla skipped away, following the path of the river. On either side were steep wooded hills, into which little cave-houses were set. The animals of Willow Valley lived in these.

Willow Valley was a very secret place. Only the animals who lived there knew their way in and out, and no one else could ever find this beautiful hidden world.

Trees of all shapes and sizes grew on

the rolling green hills. Pretty flowers danced in the meadows – daffodils and primroses, bluebells and clover, poppies in the hot summer months and snowdrops in the winter.

The air was filled with tiny wings as butterflies and ladybirds fluttered through the fields. Bright birds flew to the tops of the trees to sing to the squirrels who lived there.

Most animals lived in cave-houses. Except for the otters and water voles. *They* liked to live on the riverbank because caves were too dry for them.

Each cave-house had thick, bumpy

walls and stone floors scattered with rugs. The rooms were dark and lit with lanterns or the glow from big open fires. Curls of silvery smoke swirled out of crooked chimneys as the animals of Willow Valley were beginning their day.

Some were baking crusty bread to eat with blackberry jam. Others were sweeping and polishing their houses, now that spring had finally arrived in the valley.

"Morning!" called Martha Rabbit, as she hung her washing out to dry. Three baby bunnies bounced around her feet.

"Hello!" said Starla and Riley.

"Happy birthday Riley!" cried Mumford Mole. He was their teacher, but as today was Saturday, he wasn't at the school. As he bent down to collect his newspaper off the doorstep, his small round spectacles slipped down his shiny black nose.

"Thanks, Mr Mole!" replied Riley. "See you later!"

Riley and Starla shot under a hedge and through a field of daffodils. Then they hurried uphill, through Bluebell Wood, and down into Buttercup Meadow. "Nearly there!" Starla exclaimed.

"*I know*," panted Riley.

On the far side of the meadow stood

a line of ten ancient oak trees, like an army of ugly giants, twisted and tall.

"Follow me!" called Riley, darting between two trees.

"Ten Oaks Field!" cheered Starla. They'd arrived!

They threw themselves on to the cool grass, shut their eyes and felt the world spin. Then Riley got out his flask and they each had a drink.

"Right!" beamed Starla, getting to her feet. "Ready to go treasure hunting?"

"Yep!" said Riley, leaping up too.

He switched on his metal detector and it gave a low *buzzzzz*. Then a row of bright blue lights flashed along its front.

After a moment, these lights went out and two more buzzes sounded. "I think it's ready!" said Riley. "Right, here goes. . ."

They took it in turns to search the field, swapping over when their arms got tired. It was quite hard work but very exciting too!

When they'd searched about half the field, Riley began to feel peckish. He placed the metal detector down and they sat on a nearby tree stump. Then he took out the jam jar of goodies he'd packed for lunch.

"I can't wait for your party!" said Starla. "But I still haven't got you a present. I wanted to ask if there's anything you'd *really* like?"

"Aaaa. . ." said Riley, his mouth crammed with berries. "Ou cug get me a—"

But suddenly Riley stopped and his big round ears gave a twitch. He swallowed hard. *"Listen!"* he gasped. "The metal detector . . . it's *beeping*!"

As he leapt off the tree stump, Riley could hardly believe his luck. "Hey, Starla!" he cried. "I think we've found treasure!"

He raced over to the metal detector. *"Oooo!"* he squeaked, picking it up. "Lights! Green lights! *Everywhere!*"

All along the front of the metal detector tiny green lights were flashing. Starla scurried across. "You're right!" she gasped. "But there's no *grass*. Look – there."

She pointed at the ground where the metal detector had been. It looked like it had been dug over *very recently*.

"Who cares?" cried Riley, excitedly.

"There's treasure under here! Pass me over my rucksack! *Quick!*"

Starla handed it to him. Riley pulled out his spade and frantically started digging.

"Wait!" cried Starla. "I can help!" She knelt down beside him and started scraping at the soil with her long claws.

"This is fun!" she said with a little giggle.

Riley joined back in with the digging, being careful of Starla's paws until suddenly, his spade hit something. It was hard and it sounded like tin. "There's definitely something down here!" he panted.

"Ooo!" squealed Starla. "What?"

Riley brushed off the soil. A light grey tin appeared. *"Whoa!"* he cried. *"Look! A treasure chest!"*

Carefully, he edged it out of the ground and placed it down beside him. "I wonder what's inside?" he said.

He gripped the lid with his tiny paws and prised open the tin.

"Look!" he cried. "A sailing boat! And it's *just* like Horatio Spark's!"

"R-really?" gasped Starla, but Riley was right. The boat looked *exactly* like the one belonging to their hedgehog friend, Horatio. Riley had wanted a boat like Horatio's for ages.

He put down the tin and took out the boat. It had a polished wooden hull and off-white sails. A tiny red triangular flag fluttered at the top of its mast. *"Wow!"* gasped Riley. This boat was going to zoom like the wind!

Starla pointed out some stains on the
sails. "I don't care!" said Riley. "Horatio's
boat's got stains too. It's great!"

Riley smiled. Now he and Horatio
could race their boats on the river.
"Come on," he said. "Let's go and show
Horatio my treasure!"

He placed the boat back in the tin and Starla popped the lid on. "OK," she said. "But I can't stay long. I've got to help get your party ready."

"Oh yeah," grinned Riley. "My party!" He'd almost forgotten.

As they headed off through the field, Starla glanced back to the very spot where they'd found Riley's treasure. She had a feeling it hadn't been buried there for long.

"Come on!" cried Riley, racing on ahead.

"OK," called Starla. *"Wait for me!"*

Chapter 3

As they reached the giant oak trees, Riley was still smiling. He'd found *real* treasure on his very first expedition!

Starla led them into Buttercup Meadow and they trailed through the long grass, talking excitedly about Riley's party.

Parties in Willow Valley were always great fun. Everyone gathered, sometimes in Bluebell Wood or on one of the narrowboats, and they'd dance and play games and share delicious food.

The rabbits always made fairy cakes and the badgers brought freshly baked bread. The moles cooked pasties filled with carrots and swede while the otters made soup – watercress soup – the best in the whole of Willow Valley! The hedgehogs baked fine ginger biscuits. The squirrels made tasty nut loaves. The mice brought cheeses of all shapes and sizes! And finally, the water voles brought lemonade, so fizzy it gave you hiccups!

"What games will you have?" asked Starla.

"Loads!" Riley cried. "Pass-the-parcel, I *love* that one! And Mum said she's going to wrap up a special prize."

They wriggled under a hawthorn hedge then passed Mossy Hollow, a sheltered spot at the foot of the hills where they often came for picnics with Horatio. Suddenly Riley thought about his friend. Soon they'd be racing their boats on the river together!

Climbing uphill, they hurried on into Bluebell Wood, now a velvety carpet of soft green leaves. In a few weeks' time, when the bluebells came out, everyone would race here after school to play hide-and-seek. Riley always found the best places to hide because he was the smallest.

"Come on!" said Starla, suddenly. "Race you to Horatio's!" They scurried out of Bluebell Wood, down a steep hill, and didn't stop running until they reached the river.

Panting, they followed its twisty path to the small village square, where their school now stood empty until after the weekend.

In the middle of the square was a neat patch of grass. Here an enormous fir tree towered up. Every Christmas little candles would sit amongst its branches, twinkling down on to the snow that iced the ground below.

Riley remembered last Christmas Eve. He'd stood right here with Horatio and Starla, nibbling roasted chestnuts and trying to spot a shiny red nose in the sky!

Dotted around the village square were a few little shops. Their windows sparkled and wonderful smells drifted through their open doors.

Starla liked the baker's best, with its pretty cakes arranged in the window on dainty china stands. But Riley's favourite was the shop next door, which sold toys made from wood. This was where his grandpa, Percy Lightfoot, worked.

Beyond the square stood Horatio's cave-house, on the other side of the river. High above it grew a huge beech tree. In the autumn it rained down crunchy leaves all over Horatio's roof, making the house look like it had just grown hair – scruffy brown hair, like Riley's!

Horatio Spark was a roly-poly hedgehog and one of Riley's best friends. He had rosy red cheeks, short stumpy legs and he always seemed to be in trouble! This was not because Horatio was bad, but because he just liked to "do" things. Things that, sometimes, maybe he shouldn't do. . .

"Look!" cried Riley, peeping through the fence. Horatio was out in his garden.

"Uh oh," said Starla. "What's he up to *now*?"

"Trying to tightrope walk, I think!" sniggered Riley.

Starla opened the gate and they hurried in. "Hey, Horatio – *look*!" cried Riley, waving his tin of treasure.

"*Whoa!*" gasped Horatio. "Haaa . . . hang on a minute."

Horatio was almost up in the clouds, trying to walk across a rope he'd tied between two trees. He was clutching a frilly umbrella, which he thought might make a good parachute. Not that he was going to fall, of course!

"Eeeeeee!" squeaked Horatio, wobbling about, his arms shooting this way and that. "Don't look down, don't look down!" he chanted to himself. If *only* he'd tied the rope a tiny bit lower!

Then suddenly Horatio gave a big sneeze, dropping his parachute. "Don't *look*!" he cried as he watched the umbrella go floating to the ground. And down he tumbled after it. . .

"Catch meeeeeeeee!"

He landed upside down in a flowerpot, his fat little legs kicking wildly. "Ouch!" came a sorry, echoing voice. "I'm stuck."

Riley and Starla hurried over, each grabbing a leg to pull. "Don't worry!" called Starla. "We'll get you out!"

"I don't think we will," whispered Riley.

Finally – *pop* – out came their friend, looking a little crumpled. "Come and sit down, Horatio," said Starla kindly.

They plonked him down on a bed of toadstools and Riley fed him some berries. Almost at once, Horatio seemed much more himself.

"Just need a *bit* more practice!" he chuckled. "And maybe some plasters . . . and a helmet!" Horatio Spark never stayed sad for long.

Before Horatio could try tightrope walking again, Riley tapped his tin. "I've got something to show you," he said.

"Oooh!" cried Horatio, excitedly. "I love somethings!"

He led the way down to his den at the bottom of the garden. It was tucked behind a tatty old shed and next door to the cabbages.

Horatio spent *hours* in his den away from the many brothers and sisters he had. Only Riley and Starla were allowed to join him.

They scrambled through a tunnel

of twigs and found themselves inside.

Horatio's den looked as untidy as always.

There were comics strewn all over

the floor and conkers on frayed bits

of string. And it smelled of ginger

biscuits – one of Horatio's favourite snacks!

"Right," said Horatio, settling down

on a tree stump. "What's in the tin,

then? Let's see!"

Riley and Starla knelt on the floor.

Riley's eyes were twinkling. "I thought

you'd be out with your boat!" he said.

He glanced at Starla and smiled.

"What?" said Horatio. "But I don't

ha—"

"*Anyway*," Riley went on, "now we can sail our boats together because. . ." And he whisked the lid off the tin. "Ta daaa!"

Horatio's jaw suddenly dropped as he glimpsed the little boat. "B-but," he stuttered. "How – I mean – where? Hey, pass it over a minute."

Riley handed over the boat. "What's wrong?" asked Starla, but Horatio just gaped.

"He's just surprised!" Riley laughed. "Now that I'm an explorer, we'll find *tons* of treasure. Hey, why don't you go and get your boat and we'll race them before my party!"

Horatio blinked.

"Come on, then," beamed Riley. "Let's go!"

He went to take the boat back but Horatio held on tight. "No!" he cried. "This boat – it's mine! I buried it last night."

"You *buried* it?" Riley scratched his head. "But . . . why?"

Horatio Spark puffed out his chest. "Well," he said importantly, "I buried it for, um, a *proper* explorer to discover in a million years' time! Then they'll find my name on the sail and remember me *for ever*!"

"So, where's your name then?" Riley said quickly. "I can't see it anywhere!"

"Ah," blushed Horatio. "My pencil broke before I'd finished writing it. I started. *See* – there's a tiny dot right *there*!"

Riley tutted, but Starla knew that Horatio was telling the truth. She had wondered if the boat had been his the minute Riley had dug it up. But she hadn't known that they would both want to keep it.

Starla got slowly to her feet. She'd never seen her friends fight before. "Um, Riley," she said. "Why not leave the boat here and come and get your party ready?"

"But I *found* it!" pouted Riley. "And explorers always keep their treasure."

Horatio knew how much Riley wanted to be an explorer. He was just being mean! Besides, Horatio couldn't have wanted the boat *that* much if he was just going to leave it buried for a million years!

For a few moments nobody spoke. Then suddenly Horatio turned away and the boat slipped from his paws. Without even thinking, Riley grabbed it.

"I only want to *sail* it!" he cried, scrambling to the doorway. "Come with me, Horatio! We can share it!"

"*No!*" cried Horatio, his cheeks growing pink. "It's mine!'

He dived at Riley, who zipped away through the tunnel of twigs. "Hey!" yelled Horatio, crossly. "*Give it back!*"

He thumped off after him and Starla hurried behind, clutching Riley's metal detector and rucksack. They were just in time to see the tip of Riley's tail disappear under the gate. "Don't worry, he'll come back," said Starla.

"I don't care!" Horatio scowled. "He's not my friend any more!"

Chapter 4

When Starla found Riley again, he'd just reached the river. She passed him his things. "There," she said quietly.

"I just want to sail the boat!" muttered Riley. He blinked as a sudden gust of wind flattened his sticky-up hair. He was thinking about Horatio. So was Starla.

She glanced down at the little boat tucked under Riley's arm. "Um, well, I'd better be going," she said.

"Wait!" cried Riley. "Can't you stay?
You can help sail Horatio's – I mean –
my boat."

Riley's eyes were big and wide, like
two shiny blackcurrants. *"Please,"* he
said, his tiny pink nose twitching.

Starla thought for a minute, then
shook her head. "I have to decorate the
Whirligig. And I still haven't got you
a present. But. . ." And a grin spread
across her face. "I think I know *just* the
thing!"

She turned around and skipped away.
Riley watched her go. It didn't feel right,
being all alone on his birthday.

For a moment he thought about
going back. Back to Horatio's den.
But *that* would mean giving back the
boat. . .

"No!" The word burst from his lips
and was swept away on the breeze. It
wasn't *his* fault Horatio wouldn't share.

He'd sail the boat by himself!

Riley set off along the riverbank, looking for a sheltered spot. The air was getting chillier and chillier.

Finally he stopped by a small stone bridge where he always played pooh sticks with Horatio. There was no point going any further. This would do.

Riley put down his things and listened. For a moment, he thought he heard Horatio rustling along, all sorry. But no. It was only the wind whipping the willow tree branches and the faint rumble of a waterfall in the distance.

Riley opened his rucksack, rummaged

inside and took out the ball of string.
He tied one end around the boat's mast.
He'd need to keep a hold of it when it
was in the water. Otherwise the wind
might whisk it away.

"There!" said Riley, placing the boat
on the water. He felt the string in his
paw go tight as the breeze caught the
boat's sail.

He climbed up on to the bank, gripping
the string tightly. It felt as if he were
holding a kite that wanted to fly away.

Bit by bit, Riley let the string unwind
and watched the boat judder along. The
water was choppy and the wind was

getting stronger and stronger.

Each time it gusted, the little boat pulled further and further away. Riley gripped on tight, puffing and panting as he tried to tug it back in. The string dug into his paws but he wouldn't let go.

Then suddenly – *whoosh* – a huge gust of wind sent the boat lurching forward. "Help!" cried Riley as the string was whisked from his grasp.

Before he could stop it, the end of the string disappeared under the gurgling water. "Oh no!" he cried. *What was he going to do?*

Riley paced up and down the riverbank. He needed a plan and quick! "Think!" he muttered to himself. "Think!"

Somebody had to swim to the boat before it was swept away. He could swim, but the water was quite rough today.

Then Riley remembered the otters and water voles – they were *much* better swimmers than him! They'd be able to get to the boat no problem.

"Hello?" he called. "Is there anyone there?" He hurried along the riverbank, stopping every now and then to poke his head into soggy houses. There was nobody home. Where could they be? Maybe they'd gone to the baker's? Or to play in Buttercup Meadow? Or maybe they'd all gone off for a very long swim?

Shivering, Riley stood at the water's edge. The boat was moving further away. He took a deep breath and dipped a toe in the water. Should he jump in? Should he try to save it? *"No!"* squeaked a tiny voice in his head. *"You're too small!"*

Then suddenly the wind gave a mighty *roooaaar* and Riley toppled into the water. . .

SPLASH!

The river was freezing. Riley coughed and spluttered as the water swirled around him. As he bobbed about, kicking and splashing, Riley looked for the boat. He hadn't meant to fall in but maybe he could quickly grab it. He needed to get out of this river as fast as he could!

Then suddenly, Riley glimpsed something tangled in the reeds. There it was! The boat! Now he just had to get it.

Riley kicked off through the water. It wasn't that far away. "Come on!" he spluttered, edging along. "You can do it!"

As he swam, he thought of Horatio. If Riley lost his sailing boat, they'd never be friends again. If only he hadn't taken it. If only. . .

Gritting his teeth, Riley pushed on. He was getting closer. Not much further now.

Finally, the very tips of his claws brushed the side of the boat. With a final kick, he stretched out a paw and grabbed it!

Riley tugged the boat out of the reeds but he still had to get to the riverbank. "You can do it!" he told himself again. "Just swim!'

Shivering, he started to swim round the reeds, clutching the little boat. He was almost back. Just a whisker away when . . .

whoooossshhhhh!

A giant gust of wind caught the boat's sail and swept them off down the river. Faster and faster – whirling and twirling!

"No!" cried Riley. "*HEEEELP!*"

Suddenly, a long thin willow branch whipped through the air like a fishing rod.

Riley grabbed hold with one paw, gripping the boat in the other. He closed his eyes. He'd never felt more exhausted.

Riley felt himself being dragged through the water and up on to the bank, where he lay face down and panting. But who had saved him?

Slowly, he lifted up his head, sneezed, then looked around. "Not the best day for a swim!" grinned Horatio.

"Horatio!" cried Riley. *"It's you!"*

They sat side by side on the riverbank and Riley held out the soggy boat. "Sorry," he said. "This is yours." And he handed it back to Horatio.

"I'm sorry too," said Horatio. "That's what I came down here to say. It's lucky I did!"

"I know," nodded Riley, quietly. "Shall we go back to my house? I need to get ready for my party."

"And probably dry off a bit," grinned Horatio.

Chapter 5

Riley dripped all the way home, laughing and chatting with Horatio. It felt so good to have his best friend back.

When they arrived, Riley's mum and sister were in the warm kitchen. Mimi-Rose was drawing by the fire and his mum had her back to them as she stood at the table packing baskets of goodies for the party.

Riley hoped, if he was *really* quick, he might just manage to get upstairs

before she noticed how wet he was.
Otherwise, he knew he was in for a big
telling-off.

"Hi, Mum!" he called, zipping
towards the stairs.

"Hello," whispered Horatio, tiptoeing
behind.

"Riley's drippy!" squeaked Mimi-Rose.
"Look!"

Riley stopped in his tracks as his
mum looked up.

"Riley Black-Paw!" she exclaimed,
throwing up her paws in horror.
"Goodness me – just look at you!
Where have you been?"

Horatio curled into a prickly ball and pretended he wasn't there as Riley said, "I . . . sort of . . . fell . . . in the river."

"The river!" cried his mum. "The river! Don't you *know* how dangerous that river is? The minute I let you go exploring—"

"I'm sorry!" sniffed Riley. "Don't be cross. It's my birthday."

"Well, hurry up and get dry," said his mum. "I'll take your sister down to the *Whirligig* and you two can follow behind. Don't be long or you'll miss your own party."

She picked up two heavy baskets and bustled over to the door. "And no more mischief!" she called behind her.

As soon as they'd gone, Riley quickly got ready while Horatio uncurled himself and snacked on party-food crumbs.

"Hey, Riley," he said when they were ready to leave, "don't forget your metal detector!"

"But why do I need that?" asked
Riley.

"Just in case!" shrugged Horatio and
he handed it over.

They hurried from the house and
down the garden path, cheering
excitedly. But they'd only got as far as
the garden gate when – "Ooo!" cried
Horatio. "I've just remembered – I've
got something secret to do!"

"But you'll miss my party," grumbled
Riley.

"I won't!" beamed Horatio. "I won't
be long. Don't start the food without
me!"

Horatio raced towards the village square and Riley set off to the river. The clouds had blown away and the sun was shining.

When he arrived, his ears pricked up and he gave a leap of excitement. Everything was ready for his party!

The *Whirligig* sat on the sparkly water, draped in colourful bunting. Each flag, like a little butterfly, was fluttering in the warm breeze.

Up on deck, a long table had been draped with a white linen cloth and low wooden benches had been placed around each of its sides.

All along the top of the table
sat platefuls of yummy food
amongst jugs of pretty
daffodils and
crocuses.

Mumford Mole had his fiddle and was playing a jolly tune as animals skipped from the woods and hills, carrying baskets of goodies!

"Riley!" called Starla. She was standing on deck under a big bright banner.

Happy Birthday, Riley!

it said in neatly painted letters.

Riley clambered aboard to be met by some bunnies all wanting to wish him well. Then the cabin door opened and his mum came out carrying a plate of fairy cakes topped with pink icing and cherries. "Look what the rabbits made!" she cried. "So pretty!"

She hurried to the table and popped them down between mountains of cheese and piles of pasties as a huddle of moles appeared with presents for Riley.

"What about Horatio?" whispered Starla. "Did you make friends?"

"Yes," smiled Riley. "I gave him back his boat."

"Oh goody!" cried Starla brightly.

With that, a sudden yell of "Heeeeelp!" echoed around the valley. And rolling down the hill came Horatio Spark.

"Uh oh!" said Riley, as the prickly
ball tumbled faster and faster.

"Left!" cried Starla. "Horatio! Go
LEFT!"

It was too late. With a giant bump, he
went walloping into a tree stump. "Ouch!"
said Horatio, rubbing his head. Then he

got to his feet and grinned. "Thought rolling would be faster than walking!" he shrugged. "Pfff! Silly tree stumps!"

He marched over to the boat and they helped him up on deck. "The food!" he gasped. "Have I missed the food?"

"No," said Starla, smiling.

Now that everyone had arrived, Riley's mum started the party games with hunt-the-thimble. Mimi-Rose had hidden a thimble somewhere down below deck. "Ready, steady – *GO!*" she cried and everyone scampered off to find it.

"This way!" boomed Boris, a big chunky badger.

"No, *this* way!" giggled Posy Vole.

"Look under the beds!"

"And in all the cupboards!"

"*Quick!*" squealed the bunnies.

Soon the *Whirligig* echoed with the
sound of pattering

paws as everyone darted here and there, searching for the small silver thimble.

It was only when Digby, a shy little mole, found it inside a teapot that the game finally came to an end and musical statues began.

The party whizzed by happily and before Riley knew it, it was time for the very last game.

"Pass-the-parcel!" cheered the squirrels. They *did* so love unwrapping things! Everyone sat down in big circle and then the music began.

"I hope it's an acorn," whispered Abigail Bright. "Do you think it's an acorn? I do!"

"No, silly – it's a *carrot*!" cried Bramble Bunny.

Finally, the music stopped and everybody groaned. All except Phoebe, a sweet little badger, who was clutching the parcel in her paws.

She opened it quickly. "*Ooo!*" she squealed, pulling out a small knitted duckling. "You're so cute and fluffy!" she giggled.

"Right, then," called Riley's mum, "time for the food!"

"Hooray!" cheered everyone. They scampered over to the table and began tucking in at once.

"*Fairy cakes!*" cried Horatio Spark. "Oh yum!"

Soon Riley's plate was piled high with pasties and big chunks of cheese. But Horatio's was piled even higher with a bit of everything!

After the food came the dancing. Mumford struck up a tune on his fiddle, and Willoughby White-Whiskers joined in on an old tin whistle.

As the dancing began, Horatio found Riley, who was spinning Starla around. "It's time to give you my present!" he whispered. "Follow me!"

Chapter 6

Horatio found Riley's metal detector and tiptoed off the boat. "Hang on," whispered Riley, pattering behind. "Why do we need *that*?"

"Aha," nodded Horatio. "You'll see!"

"*Hey*," called Starla. "Wait for me!" She snatched up a little basket with her present for Riley inside. "Where are we going?"

"It's a secret!" grinned Horatio.

He led them off up the hill and into

Bluebell Wood. "Nearly there!" puffed Horatio. "Not much further!"

Finally, they came to a small clearing surrounded by giant fir trees. A tiny stream trickled along and the air was quiet and still.

"Ta daa!" beamed Horatio. He looked at Riley. "This is where I've buried your present!"

"You've *buried* my present?"

"That's right!" said Horatio. "And you'll need to find it with *this*!"

He handed Riley the metal detector. Riley scratched his head. He peered around. Where should he begin?

Suddenly he spotted some small
wooden signs that had been hammered
into the ground. They were set out like
a treasure trail with a clue written on
each one.

"Start here and no cheating!" Riley
read aloud. Starla gave a giggle.

"Don't laugh," said Horatio. "Took me ages, this did! *That's* why I was late for the party."

He nudged Riley. "Go on then," he said. "Off you go!"

Riley switched on the metal detector and waited until it was ready. Then he hurried across to the first clue and stopped.

"Take three steps sideways," Riley read aloud. "Left or right?" he called to Horatio.

"Err, left – no, right!" Horatio called back. "Whichever way the next clue is! See – there!"

Riley took three steps to the left, where the next clue stood beside a clump of flowers.

"Count the flowers, then go forward," Riley read. Riley counted them. There were six.

"Six steps forward, then!" Horatio called over, beaming.

"Shouldn't he just go straight to the clue that says, 'the present's right here'?" Starla said.

"Ssshhh!" flapped Horatio. *Don't tell him where it is!*"

Riley tried hard not to laugh. Horatio had gone to *so* much trouble, he didn't want to hurt his feelings. He counted six steps forward, where another clue waited. "How many prickles has Horatio got? Go sideways that many!"

Riley scratched his head. "Um, Horatio," he said, "how many prickles have you got?"

"Ooo!" said Horatio. "Tricky one, that. Tons and tons, I suppose!"

"O-K," said Riley, slowly. "I'll go sideways tons and tons, then, shall I?"

"Yep!" grinned Horatio. "Getting the hang of this now, aren't you?"

Riley sniggered, then started walking sideways.

"Keep going!" cried Horatio. "Just a few more steps. . ."

"Go on!" cried Starla, clapping her paws. "Go, Riley!"

Finally, Riley reached the sign that said, The Present's RIGHT HERE↓.

"I think I'm getting close," he grinned.

"You are!" cried Horatio. *"Really* close!"

Suddenly, *beeeeep* went the metal detector, and tiny green lights started flashing. "You've done it! *Hooray!"* Horatio cheered.

"Yeah!" laughed Riley. "Great clues!"

He passed the metal detector to Starla and knelt down on the ground. Then he started digging with his paws as the others watched on excitedly.

Soon his paw hit something solid. "You've got it! You've got it!" Horatio cried. Riley scraped the soil away. It was a tin. A tin that looked *very* familiar. . .

"Take the lid off, then!" Horatio smiled. Riley edged it off slowly. Inside was Horatio's sailing boat with a tag round its mast that said, *To my best friend, Riley!*

"But, Horatio," said Riley, "this your boat."

"I want you to have it!" cried Horatio.

"I *did* have this HUGE ginger cake
to give you. It was soft! And sweet!
And gooey! Anyway, it sort of . . .
disappeared." He glanced at his tummy
and his cheeks went very pink.

Riley picked up the sailing boat but
he knew he couldn't keep it. "It's yours,"

he said. "I know how much you love it." And he handed it back to Horatio. "Just try not to bury it again!"

"OK!" smiled Horatio. "If you're sure. But you can borrow it anytime you like."

With that, Riley felt a tap on his shoulder. "You've got *one* more present to open," said Starla. "Remember?"

She lifted it out of her basket and handed it to Riley. It was beautifully wrapped and tied with a big yellow ribbon.

Riley's eyes lit up at once. "Thanks, Starla!" he said. He pulled off the ribbon and unfolded the leaves.

"Wow!" he gasped as he lifted up a sailing boat with a tiny *blue* flag. "How? I mean, who?"

"It belonged to my grandfather!" Starla smiled. "I didn't know what to get you, but then, when I left you by the river, I remembered his boat! So I asked him if I could give it to you."

"Thanks!" cried Riley. He could hardly believe it. Willoughby White-Whiskers had given *him* his boat!

"He knows you'll look after it," Starla said.

"I will!" nodded Riley, stroking its sail. *"Always. . ."*

Suddenly, Horatio clapped his paws. "Right," he cried. "Let's get back to the party! My tummy says it's time for birthday cake!"

They ran all the way back to the *Whirligig*. When they got there, Riley found Starla's grandfather. "Thanks for the boat, Mr White-Whiskers!" he said, and Willoughby White-Whiskers smiled.

"Just have fun with it, my boy!"

"I will!" cried Riley. "So much fun! And I'll treasure it for ever."

At that moment, Riley's mum appeared carrying a *huge* birthday cake. It was in the shape of an explorer's map and had lots of flickering candles. Then everybody gathered around to sing happy birthday to Riley.

Happy Birthday to you,
Happy Birthday to you,

Happy Birthday dear Riley!
Happy Birthday to you!
Hip Hip Hooray!

When the party was finally over, Riley walked home with his mum and sister, the boat tucked under his arm. Tomorrow he'd take it to Bluebell Wood and race it on the stream with Horatio.

Before he went to sleep that night, he placed the boat on his window ledge, then clambered into bed. Silver ribbons of moonlight lit its off-white sails and the little blue flag sitting at the top of the mast.

Riley closed his eyes and sailed away
into his happy dreams. This would be
one birthday he'd never, *ever* forget. . .